Tales
from the
SANDLOT
#3

The Catcher Who Shocked the World

by Dan Gutman

Illustrated by Robert Papp

AN
APPLE
PAPERBACK

SCHOLASTIC INC.

New York   Toronto   London   Auckland   Sydney

No part of this publication may be reproduced in whole or in part, or stored in a retrieval system, or transmitted in any form or by any means, electronic, mechanical, photocopying, recording, or otherwise, without written permission of the publisher. For information regarding permission, write to Scholastic Inc., 555 Broadway, New York, NY 10012.

ISBN 0-590-13762-X

Text copyright © 1997 by Dan Gutman. Illustrations copyright © 1997 by Scholastic Inc. All rights reserved. Published by Scholastic Inc. APPLE PAPERBACKS and the APPLE PAPERBACKS logo are trademarks and/or registered trademarks of Scholastic Inc.

12 11 10 9 8 7 6 5 4 3 2 1   7 8 9/9 0 1 2/0

Printed in the U.S.A.   40

First Scholastic printing, June 1997

To Rachel Trotta

THE ST. CLOUD TORNADOES*

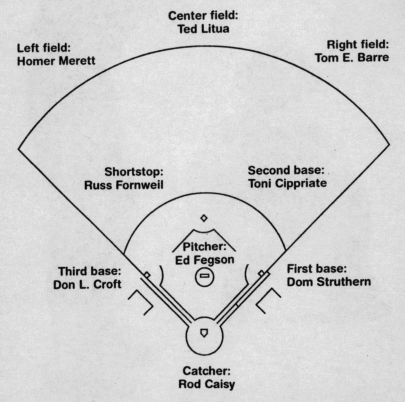

Center field:
Ted Litua

Left field:
Homer Merett

Right field:
Tom E. Barre

Shortstop:
Russ Fornweil

Second base:
Toni Cippriate

Pitcher:
Ed Fegson

Third base:
Don L. Croft

First base:
Dom Struthern

Catcher:
Rod Caisy

*The names of all the Tornadoes are scrambled versions of common weather terms. For instance, the letters in the name of shortstop Russ Fornweil can be rearranged to make "SNOW FLURRIES." Can you unscramble the names of the other Tornadoes? The answers are in the back of the book.

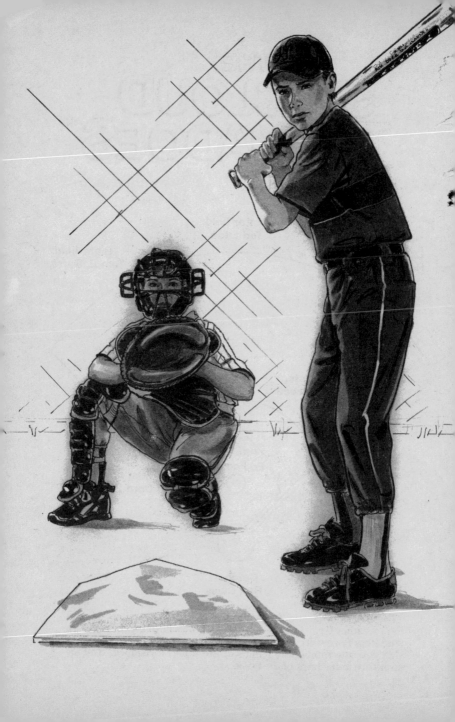

Rod the Clod

I never wanted to be a catcher. Who does?

Catching is a weird position. You wear strange equipment that none of the other players has to wear. You're the only one on the field who plays in foul territory. You face the opposite direction from everyone else on your team.

You squat.

On the other hand, the catcher is a Little League team's leader. You're like a football team's quarterback. The coach may shout orders from the bench, but on the field, the catcher is in charge.

There's so much you have to do. You have to call pitches, block the plate, and throw out base stealers. You have to know which hitters like the ball high in the strike zone and which ones can't hit a curveball. You've got to be alert all the time. You've got to be able to make decisions quickly.

You've got to use your head.

The biggest, heaviest, toughest, and slowest kid is usually picked to catch. Okay, I admit it. I'm big, heavy, tough, and slow. And I wanted to play baseball. So I became a catcher.

My name is Rod Caisy. Some kids call me Rod the Clod, but not to my face because they know I'd beat them up. I play for the Tornadoes, a Little League team in St. Cloud, Florida. If you've ever been to Disney World, St. Cloud is about twenty miles south of Orlando.

This is my story. You may find it a bit . . . let me see, how can I put this?

I know. You may find it a bit *shocking*.

Steady Eddie, Claude, and the Winchell Factor

It was getting toward the end of the school year, and it was a really hot, muggy afternoon. Nobody wants to play ball in this weather, but here in central Florida you don't have a lot of choice.

My chest protector, catcher's mask, and shin guards were sticking to me. I was really uncomfortable.

But we were in the sixth inning, the last inning. *Just a few more minutes,* I thought to myself. *Then I can go home and take a nice long shower.*

A rumble of thunder echoed in the distance.

I hate to admit it, but the Tornadoes are the

3

worst team in our league. Pitching is our problem. We don't really have any.

Ed Fegson is my best friend, but he'll be the first to tell you he's no Nolan Ryan. Eddie's a junk-baller. He throws so soft his pitches could barely break a pane of glass. But he could hit the glass if he wanted to, that's for sure. Eddie has pinpoint control. That's why we call him Steady Eddie.

We were playing the Hurricanes, the best team in our league. Usually they cream us, but by some miracle we had a 2–1 lead. Eddie got the first two Hurricanes out, and I trotted out to the mound to give him a pep talk.

"Okay, one more out and we've got these bums," I said, putting my arm on Eddie's shoulder while glancing toward the plate to see who was up next. "This guy couldn't hit the ball if we put it on a tee."

"It ain't over till it's over, Rod," Eddie replied nervously.

Steady Eddie doesn't exactly overflow with confidence. He tends to assume the worst is going to happen in any situation. I have to keep trying to convince him to look on the bright side.

A kid named Claude Powers stepped up to the plate for the Hurricanes. He's kind of famous

around here because his dad is on TV every night. Mr. Powers is the weatherman on Channel 6 in Orlando. Claude can't play ball for beans, but I think his dad makes him.

Claude is in my science class at school, and he's one of those genius nerds. He likes to take apart junky old appliances and build weird machines out of them. He wins first prize in the science fair every year with some goofy exhibit.

Once, Claude got into trouble when he used his computer to break into the telephone system. He programmed it so that when people picked up their home phone, a voice would come on and say, "Please deposit twenty cents." That was Claude Powers' idea of fun.

What would you expect from a kid named Claude? I thought to myself as Claude Powers stepped into the batter's box.

As he took his stance, I glanced upward. Clouds had started filling in the blue sky. They were billowing upward really high. The wall of clouds overhead looked like a giant anvil hovering over the field. I'm not really into weather or anything, but this was an awesome sight.

"Finished daydreaming, Rod?" grumbled the umpire behind me. "I wanna get this game finished before it starts raining."

Rich Winchell umps most of our games. He's an okay guy, but even on nice days, Winch wants to get the game over with as quickly as possible. So if a pitch is anywhere close to the plate, he'll almost always call it a strike.

When he's umping our games, I always take "the Winchell factor" into account. In other words, swing at anything.

"What's the rush, Winch?" I asked, settling into my crouch. "Afraid you'll melt?"

As Steady Eddie pumped strike one over the plate and Claude took a wild swing at it, I couldn't stop staring at the sky. The top of the cloud appeared to be white and flat, while the bottom was getting darker.

I noticed that the air was suddenly cooler, more comfortable. A breeze drifted around the field. It felt good.

Eddie delivered the next pitch. It was about a foot outside and I had to reach for it.

"Strike two!" yelled Winchell.

"What!?" complained Claude. "That pitch was in the next *county*!"

"Looked good to me," Winchell replied.

I kept my mouth shut. One more strike and we would actually beat the Hurricanes. A few raindrops tapped against my helmet.

"I think I'm gonna havta call the game," Winchell muttered.

"Oh, come on, Winch," I protested. "It's just a few drops. One more pitch and you can go home."

We don't get too worked up over a few raindrops around here. Florida has more thunderstorms than any state in the United States. Winchell motioned for Eddie to pitch. I called for a fastball, up high in the strike zone.

As Eddie started his windup, I caught a whiff of sulfur in the air. I felt the hair on my arms standing on end.

The pitch was right where I wanted it and Claude took a healthy cut. He got a piece of it, but he swung under the ball. It sailed almost straight up in the air, very high.

"I got it!" I shouted.

This is the ball game, I said to myself.

I tossed my mask aside and looked up. It was easy to see the white ball against the dark cloud overhead.

The wind had picked up and it was pushing the ball backward, into foul territory behind the plate. I knew I only had about ten feet of dirt behind me before the chain-link backstop would block my path.

There wasn't enough time to run around behind the backstop to catch the ball. Instead, I took a few steps backward and dug my sneaker into the fence. The ball had reached its highest point and was starting to come down. I was watching it as I dug my other sneaker into the fence and began to climb the backstop.

I made it to the top and positioned myself to make the catch. The wind howled. The ball was plummeting earthward. I stuck my mitt up to reach for it.

"Rod! Look out!" Eddie yelled.

An ear-splitting, buzzing, humming noise filled the air over the diamond. A blast, like the roar of a furnace, rocked me. At that instant, a bolt of lightning burst from the bottom of the cloud.

It was a thin, bold, beautiful, and terrifying light, whiter than anything I'd ever seen. There was an orange tinge around it. I had to close my eyes, it was so bright. I've been to Fourth of July fireworks as far back as I can remember. But they were never anything like *this*.

Everybody knows lightning strikes the highest object in an area, and the falling baseball was the highest thing on the field. The bolt zapped the ball and continued downward, hitting the backstop I was clinging to. At the same instant, there was a sound like cloth tearing and the crack of thunder.

The sky seemed to rip apart. It was like the world *exploded*.

That was the last thing I remembered.

Lightning Rod

Later, my teammates told me what happened. I have to believe they were telling the truth.

My entire body lit up, they said. The bolt of lightning passed through me and knocked my left sneaker off my foot.

The muscles in my arms and legs jerked. That propelled me off the backstop and flung me through the air until I landed on the grass halfway to the pitcher's mound. I lay there for a few minutes without moving.

"Rod's dead!" Eddie wailed as the whole team rushed to my side.

I knew I wasn't dead. If I was dead, I wouldn't have heard them talking about me.

"Somebody get a doctor!" shouted Winchell.

"Get a blanket!" our second baseman, Toni Cippriate, screamed. "Keep him warm!"

"Don't touch him!" cautioned Dom Struthern, our first baseman. "He's like a live wire! You might get electrocuted yourself!"

Lying there, I noticed the air smelled fresh and cool. I knew I couldn't be dead, because dead people don't smell. Well, I guess they do *smell*, but, I mean, they *can't* smell.

Oh, you know what I mean.

I figured the breath had been knocked out of me. I felt a tingly feeling all over except for my legs, which were totally numb. I was afraid to move. I was afraid that if I *tried* to move I might not be able to. I was afraid I might be paralyzed.

"Who . . . won?" I asked, opening my eyes. Everybody gasped.

"We did," said Eddie, leaning over me. "You caught the ball."

Eddie took the ball out of my mitt and held it in front of my face. It was hideously scorched on one side, with smoke still curling up from it.

"We actually beat the Hurricanes?" I asked.

"I didn't think it was possible," Eddie said.

He told me what happened. Everybody was amazed that I had survived the bolt of lightning.

"How do you feel, Rod?" Eddie asked, cradling my head.

I thought about that question for a few seconds as I lay there. My body felt strong, like my muscles had been removed and replaced with newer, stronger ones. My head was clear, like a plumber had gone inside and cleaned out all the clogged pipes. Feeling was slowly returning to my legs.

"I feel . . . great!" I finally announced.

"I guess nobody can call you 'Rod the Clod' anymore," said Eddie. "From now on, we're going to have to call you 'Lightning Rod.'"

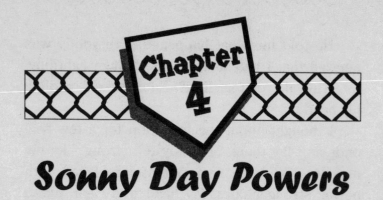

Chapter 4

Sonny Day Powers

"Stand back!" a man's voice shouted just as I was about to get up off the grass.

The next thing I knew some guy was on top of me, pinching my nostrils closed with his fingers while blowing air into my mouth.

"Get *off* me!" I sputtered, struggling to turn my face away from his.

I could tell right away it was Claude Powers' dad, the famous weatherman Sonny Day Powers. He's a big, nerdy-looking guy, sort of a grown-up version of his nerdy son.

From what I've heard, his name really *is* Sonny Day Powers. When he and his wife had a baby, Sonny wanted to name the baby Cloudy so the two of them could be Sunny Day and Cloudy

Day. Sonny's wife apparently threatened to divorce him, so they compromised. They named the baby Claude Everett Day Powers.

Claude E. Day, get it?

It should come as no surprise that Sonny Day Powers is known around the Orlando area as "the wacky weatherman."

I wasn't sure which was worse, getting hit by lightning, or having Sonny Day Powers' mouth against mine. The important thing was that I was alive. The thundercloud had moved past the field, and the sky looked like it was clearing up.

"That was some shock you took," Sonny said as he helped me to my feet. "How about coming on the news with me tomorrow night and telling people what it felt like to survive a lightning bolt?"

"Gee, I don't know," I stammered. "I won't have anything to say."

"Sure you will!" Sonny insisted. "And it will give me a good opportunity to tell the viewers what *they* can do to avoid getting hit by lightning themselves."

Reluctantly, I agreed to be interviewed on TV.

Sonny told me he would send a taxi to pick me up the next day. Then he walked off the field with his son Claude.

I started packing up my equipment to go home. My mitt was a little scorched around the edges, but it was still usable. *It will be cool,* I thought, *to play ball with a mitt that has been struck by lightning.*

My chest protector was burned with crisscrossing lines, like a frozen waffle that had been left in the toaster too long. Looking at the backstop I could see that the lines on my chest protector matched the pattern of the fence.

The chest protector may have actually protected my chest, it occurred to me. *Maybe it saved my life.*

As I was putting my gear into my duffel bag, I noticed a funny feeling in the back of my head. It wasn't pain. It was more like some kind of a vibration back there. It was like nothing I had ever experienced before.

My bat! I almost forgot my bat!

I went back to the bench to get it. There were a bunch of aluminum bats lined up on the grass there. I got down on my hands and knees to see

16

which one was mine. After a few seconds I spotted it.

I was about to pick the bat up, but something stopped me. I stared at the bat. It almost seemed to move, very slightly. I stared at it some more.

And then, as I stared at my bat, slowly but perceptibly, the bat began to *bend*.

"Look at that!" Eddie said, and all my teammates gathered around.

Like a long piece of Play-Doh, the bat slowly molded itself until it was almost the shape of a letter L. When I stopped staring at it, it stopped bending.

My teammates looked at me with a combination of astonishment and fear in their faces.

Chapter 5

PK

Just as Sonny promised, the taxi pulled up outside
my house to bring me to the Channel 6 studios.
Mom had to do some work in her office at home
and she said it was okay for me to go to Orlando
by myself as long as I was being escorted there
and back.

I had never been inside a television studio before. It was pretty cool. On TV, it looks as if they
do the news in a huge room. But when I saw it
in person, the studio was just a couple of desks
with a painted background behind it and some
big TV cameras in front.

Sonny Day Powers was already on the air. As
he wrapped up the weather report, a fast-motion
video of billowing storm clouds was projected on
the screen behind him.

"That's our five day forecast, Orlando," Sonny said. "And now I have a special treat for all you weather watchers who were caught in that sudden thunderstorm yesterday. Did you ever wonder what causes lightning? Well, I'll tell you. Moist air near the ground rises and mingles with colder air above. This creates an enormous thundercloud, which may be thirteen miles high. It's called a *cumulonimbus* cloud. I love the sound of that word, don't you? Let's all say cumulonimbus together."

The news anchor, the sports guy, and the camera crew all repeated *"Cumulonimbus!"*

"Good!" Sonny continued enthusiastically. "Inside that cloud, raindrops and ice particles bump and rub against each other. This causes static electricity. The top of the cloud becomes positively charged and the bottom becomes negatively charged. Electricity builds up, and — *ZAP!* — a spark gets launched at ninety thousand miles a second from the cloud to the ground below it. That's what lightning is, basically. An electrical spark from a thundercloud."

A stagehand on the scaffold above Sonny dropped a foam lightning bolt on Sonny's head.

"Ouch!" he said, falling to the floor. "I'm shocked!"

Then the stagehand dropped a bucket of water on Sonny's head, drenching him. Sonny shook all over like a big dog after a bath. Then he continued. . . .

"What about thunder? Well, thunder is caused because the lightning bolt heats the air in its path. The air expands explosively and generates sound waves."

Off camera, somebody took a big sheet of metal and whacked it with a hammer. It made a loud crashing noise that sounded at least a little like thunder. Sonny made a funny face and started staggering around the studio like a zombie in a bad horror movie.

"I gotta switch to doing the sports!" he moaned. "This weather stuff is too dangerous!"

While Sonny was doing his thing, a lady led me over to a chair on the set and attached a microphone to my shirt.

"I'd like to introduce a young man from St. Cloud named Rod Caisy," Sonny said.

I noticed a red light lit up on the TV camera pointing at me.

"They call him Lightning Rod. When the thunderstorm hit yesterday, my son Claude was at bat in a Little League game. Claude hit a high pop-up and Rod here was the catcher. Just as he caught the ball, he was struck my lightning. As you can see, he survived it. Rod, tell us, what did it feel like?"

"I don't remember very much," I explained. "As the ball was going up, I thought the only way to catch it would be to climb the backstop. Then this light came out of the sky. It was like a blinding flashbulb right in my face. It knocked me off the backstop and threw me almost all the way to the pitcher's mound. I guess I'm lucky to be alive."

"You *are* lucky to be alive," Sonny said. "About a hundred people are killed in the United States each year by lightning. Were you scared, Rod?"

"Afterward I was, yeah. I thought I might be paralyzed or something."

"Tell me, Rod. What do you think you *should* have done when the storm arrived?"

"I think maybe I should have called for a sinkerball instead of a high fastball," I said. "Then your son Claude would have hit the ball on the ground instead of popping up."

Sonny laughed before turning back toward the camera.

"I have some other advice for all you viewers," he said. "If you see a thundercloud forming, get inside right away! Or at least get in a car. If you can't go inside, *don't* take shelter under a tree, on a hilltop, on the beach, or *especially* on a metal backstop. Find a valley, and crouch low to the ground. Lightning usually strikes the highest point in an area. If you have shoes that have metal in them, take them off. And here's a little tip. Rod, do you know how to tell how far away a thunderstorm is?"

"I have no idea," I admitted.

"Just count the number of seconds between the lightning bolt and the thunderclap. It takes five seconds for the sound of thunder to travel one mile. So if you count five seconds between the lightning and the thunder, the storm is a mile away. Ten seconds and it's two miles away. Well, that's our weather for tonight. Remember, every cloud has a silver lining."

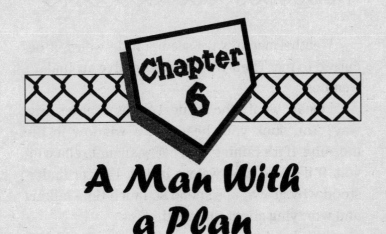

A Man With a Plan

We peeled off our microphones and Sonny escorted me down the hall. Inside his office, the walls were jammed with posters of clouds, storms, floods, tornadoes, and hurricanes. On his shelves were a bunch of weathervanes, thermometers, and other weather instruments. Books about weather were scattered around the room.

There were some photos on Sonny's desk. I expected them to be pictures of Sonny's wife and his son Claude, but when I took a close look I saw they were autographed pictures of famous weathermen.

Everything in the office had something to do with weather!

Weathermen always seem a little weird, it occurred to me. Their whole lives revolve around . . . weather.

I mean, what's the big deal about weather, anyway? You stick your head out a window in the morning. If it's raining, you carry an umbrella with you. If it's cold, you wear a jacket. I never understood why grown-ups spend so much time talking and worrying about the weather.

Still, I didn't want to insult Sonny. I told him his stuff was cool, especially the weather instruments.

"You know the old saying," he said, picking up a globe and spinning it slowly as he stared at it. "Everybody talks about the weather, but nobody ever *does* anything about it. Well, Rod, I intend to *do* something about the weather."

"What are you going to do about it?" I asked, curiously.

"I'm sort of an amateur scientist in my spare time," he said, holding the globe in his hands like it was a crystal ball. "Imagine, Rod. The air around a lightning bolt is hotter than fifty thousand degrees. That's five times the temperature on the surface of the sun!"

I felt like asking, "What's your point?" but restrained myself.

"Rod, did you ever have a toy or game that was powered by a nine-volt battery?"

"Sure," I replied.

"Well, when you got hit by that lightning bolt, you got zapped with a hundred and twenty-five *million* volts. A large thunderstorm releases as much energy as a megaton bomb."

"Wow!" I said, genuinely impressed.

"Every day there are forty-four thousand thunderstorms around the globe, Rod. Every *second*, one hundred lightning bolts strike our planet. That's eight million a day. Lightning gives off more energy than all the electric generators in the United States *combined*. If we could store this energy, we wouldn't need gas, coal, nuclear, or solar power."

"So lightning could be the answer to all our energy problems?" I asked.

"Exactly! And we would have no pollution, no damage to the environment, and no more dependence on foreign oil!"

"So why haven't we done that?" I asked.

"Two problems, Rod," Sonny explained. "First, a bolt of lightning only lasts one ten-thousandth of a second. It comes and goes too fast. Second, lightning is like a giant gorilla. It goes wherever it likes, and we can't predict where it's going to go next."

The guy seemed to be a little nutty, but he also made a certain amount of sense. I knew from school that human beings are rapidly using up the earth's natural resources. Someday there won't be any more oil to drill or coal to dig. Maybe the energy of lightning *could* be the answer to our problem.

"Rod," Sonny said, putting down the globe and looking at me seriously, "I have a plan to harness the power of lightning."

"How are you going to do that?"

"Did you ever hear of PK, Rod?"

"PK?" I asked, "No, what's that?"

"PK stands of psychokinesis. 'Psycho' means mind. 'Kinesis' means position. PK is movement by the mind. It's the ability to move objects using only the power of the mind."

I thought about how I bent the baseball bat after I had been struck by lightning. Except for my teammates, nobody knew about it.

"Moving objects with your mind?" I said nervously. "That sounds crazy."

"Maybe it is and maybe it *isn't*," Sonny said. "Back in the 1970s, an Israeli man named Uri Geller amazed audiences by taking ordinary metal objects — like spoons and nails — and bending them just by *looking* at them. It was said he could change the molecular structure of the metal to make objects bend."

"What does that have to do with *me?*" I asked, even though I had a good idea what the answer would be.

"Uri Geller said he got this power after he received a severe electrical shock in a childhood accident. Rod, I believe there is something about electricity going through the human body that can give a person PK. You got a pretty good jolt of juice yesterday. I'd like to test you to see if *you* have PK."

I want to see the world's energy problems solved as much as the next kid. But I don't want to be anybody's guinea pig. *Sonny Day Powers might be totally insane*, I thought to myself. Maybe he wanted to hook me up to some machine and zap me with electric shocks.

"Even if I had PK," I asked, "why would bending spoons solve the energy problem?"

"That's just the beginning, Rod! If you could bend a spoon, you could bend steel. If you could bend steel, you could bend guns so they wouldn't shoot. You could steer nuclear missiles away from populated areas. You could open the strongest locks. You could disrupt navigation and communication devices. Armies would be powerless against you."

Sonny was getting more and more worked up as he spoke. I backed away from him. He must have seen the look of fear in my eyes, because suddenly Sonny calmed down and backed off a little.

"Rod, half of all forest fires are ignited by lightning."

"So you mean a person might be able to move a lightning bolt away from a tree using the power of his mind?" I asked.

"Not *any* person!" Sonny exclaimed. "*You*, Rod! Only *you* can prevent forest fires!"

With that, he let out a loud, cackling laugh.

"We must control lightning and not let it control *us*," he continued, moving toward me again. "The person who can harness the power of lightning can rule the *world*!"

Quickly, Sonny strode over to the blackboard and wrote these words on it:

LOW PRESSURE

"If you scramble those letters, Rod, do you know what you can spell?"

I looked at the words LOW PRESSURE and tried to form other words that would use the same letters. When Sonny saw I was struggling, he wrote this on the blackboard:

POWERS RULES!

Then he looked at me with a devilish grin.

Sonny Day Powers was totally nuts, I thought to myself. He actually thinks that because LOW PRESSURE is an anagram of POWERS RULES, he's destined to rule the world!

Man, somebody must have dropped a barometer on Sonny Day Powers' head! I'd seen enough science fiction movies to know a crazy person when I met one. Sonny had a gleam in his eye that was a dead giveaway.

I decided right then and there that I wasn't going to tell him about how I bent the baseball bat. The wacky weatherman was a dangerous lunatic.

"I should really be going," I said, backing toward the door. "Thanks for putting me on TV."

"Not so fast, Rod."

He got in the way of the door and put an arm around my shoulder. He steered me over to his desk. On the surface were a bunch of paper clips, nails, tacks, a can opener, and other small metal objects. Sonny sat me in his desk chair and peered at me from the other side of the desk.

"See if you can move any of these objects, Rod," Sonny instructed.

I reached over and pushed a paper clip a few inches.

"No, not with your hand," he said. "With your *mind.*"

I didn't know how powerful my PK was. But if I could bend a baseball bat, bending a paper clip would be *easy.* I didn't want Sonny to know that, though. I tried to turn off my brain and not think about bending any metal.

That didn't work. As soon as I tried *not* to think about bending metal, all I could think about was bending metal. *I've got to think about some-thing completely different*, I said to myself.

I decided to think about baseball. A game situation. *It was the fourth inning*, I imagined. *We had the bases loaded. There were two outs. The count was one and one. The score was 4–3. The wind was blowing toward left field. The runners took their leads. The catcher flashed a sign. The pitcher went into his windup . . .*

Sonny broke my concentration with a sigh. None of the metal objects had bent or moved.

"I guess that bolt of lightning didn't give you PK after all," he said dejectedly. "Too bad. I had such high hopes."

"Sorry, Mr. Powers," I said, relieved.

I decided that as soon as I got out of the studio I would avoid Sonny Day Powers as much as possible.

Sonny led me out of his office. As we stood by the door, he reached into his pocket and pulled out a key to lock up.

He seemed to be having trouble getting the key into the lock. He tried again, and the key still didn't fit. Sonny held the key up and peered at it.

The key was *bent*. Like my bat.

Sonny turned and looked at me. He had that wicked gleam in his eye again.

"I didn't have anything to do with that!" I protested. "You must have sat on it or something."

"Oh, no, it was *you*!" Sonny exclaimed gleefully. "Ahahahahahaha!"

That was enough for me. This guy was crazy. I turned around and ran. As I dashed down the hallway, I could still hear his voice echoing. . . .

"Do you know what Shakespeare said about lightning, Rod? He said:

'Swift as a shadow, short as any dream,
Brief as the lightning in the collied night,
That, in a spleen, unfolds both heaven and earth,
And ere a man hath power to say, "Behold!"
The jaws of darkness do devour it up!'"

When I got in the taxi, I could still hear his madman's cackle echoing through the hallway.

Mind Over Matter

Sonny Day Powers may have been out of his mind, but something was going on in *my* mind. I clearly had the power of PK.

After the taxi dropped me off at home, I went up to my room and locked the door. I looked around for metal objects and gathered a bunch of stuff on my desk. A pair of scissors. Some nails. A coathanger. My Little League trophies.

This time, I didn't think about baseball. I wanted to see how powerful my PK could be. I visualized the objects moving and bending, sliding across my desk. I tried to make them hover in the air.

It didn't work, at least not at first. *I must look really stupid*, I thought, sitting here trying to move a pair of scissors without touching it.

Then, quite suddenly, the scissors *moved*. It might have only moved a half an inch or so to the left, but it definitely moved. I hadn't jiggled the desk. There hadn't been an earthquake. I moved the scissors using only the power of my mind.

Next I worked on the nails, which are lighter and should be easier to move. In a few minutes I was able to bend them or slide them, whichever I chose. I could move them left or right, forward or back, and even at an angle.

I could take the coathanger and, without touching it, morph it into the shape of a circle, a square, even a dog. It reminded me of the way clowns make sculptures out of those skinny balloons.

The more I practiced, the better I got. Soon I was able to move larger, heavier objects. I could slide my trophies around, as if they were little people chasing each other across my desk.

It was like magic. No, it *was* magic. And I could turn it on and off like I was flipping a switch.

WATCH THIS! read the note I slipped to Eddie toward the end of history class the next day.

Mr. Kors was going on and on about King Hammurabi of Mesopotamia and I was doing all I could to keep my eyes open.

WATCH WHAT?? Eddie's return note said.

WATCH KORS CAREFULLY, I wrote back.

Then, concentrating as hard as I could, I used my PK to pull the zipper on Mr. Kors' pants down.

I looked to Eddie for a reaction and he shrugged. He hadn't seen it.

Again I concentrated on Mr. Kors' zipper. This time I pulled it up, doing it extra slowly. The zipper was about three-quarters of the way up when Eddie burst out laughing.

"Mr. Fegson," said Mr. Kors sternly. "Perhaps you would like to share with the class what's so amusing about Babylonia."

"I'm sorry, Mr. Kors," Eddie said sheepishly. "I was just wondering if the ancient Babylonians ever attempted to fly."

Nice recovery, Eddie, I thought to myself as I pulled Mr. Kors' zipper down again.

"Fly?" asked Mr. Kors. "What do you mean?"

"Well," Eddie continued, suppressing a laugh. "We've learned that several ancient civilizations attempted to build flying machines. Did the Babylonians ever try to fly?"

I pulled Mr. Kors' zipper up again. Eddie was working as hard as he could not to laugh. There were a few snickers in the class. Some kids saw what was going on.

"Fly . . . fly . . . fly . . ." mused Mr. Kors. "That's a good question, Eddie."

By that time, everybody in the class was staring at Mr. Kors' fly. I was making the zipper go up and down like a pogo stick.

Soon, kids were pounding their fists against their desks. Tears were running down their faces. One kid fell off his chair. He was holding his stomach and crawling around the floor.

The only one in the room who didn't see what was happening was Mr. Kors. He got really mad and gave our whole class detention. But it was worth it.

After school, Eddie and I had a good laugh about it over a game of pinball. He was beating me pretty badly, but in the middle of the game a thought crossed my mind: *Who needs flippers when you've got PK?*

I started moving the ball around with my mind, knocking down anything that was worth a lot of points and preventing the ball from falling between the flippers. I could have kept a single ball going forever.

"Look ma," I said to Eddie, "no hands!"

Being able to play pinball and pull down people's zippers using only the power of my mind was pretty cool. But I didn't see any practical use for the power of PK

At least not right away.

Shutting Up the Bombers

We had a game the next day against the Bombers. Everybody in our league knows the Bombers are a bunch of jerks. At the end of their games, when we all get in line to shake hands with the other team, the Bombers grab your hand and squeeze it as hard as they can. That's the kind of jerks they are.

Steady Eddie was on the mound. Winchell was our ump again. He must have been in a real hurry to get home, because he was calling *everything* a strike. I told Eddie to miss the strike zone on purpose, and the Bombers were striking out left and right because of Winch's bad calls.

The Bombers were better than us, but they had only scored two runs because it took them five innings to realize they should swing at anything. We managed to score three runs ourselves. So in the last inning it was 3–2 in favor of the Tornadoes.

There were no outs and a runner on first when this . . . *thing* stepped up to the plate. The guy was truly enormous and scary-looking. He reminded me of those Neanderthal men we learned about in social studies.

I knew Eddie would take one look at the guy and go into a panic. I jogged out to the mound to calm him down.

"Look at that kid!" Eddie whispered. "He's bigger than my dad! What is he, a mutant?"

"Calm down, Eddie."

"We're dead, Rod. That guy is going to take me over the wall and win the game. I just know it."

"Knock it off," I said. "You can get this caveman out. He's just another kid. He puts on his pants one leg at a time, just like you and me."

"Yeah, but he gets his pants from the big and tall man's shop!" Eddie whined.

"Stop worrying. I have a plan."

To be honest, there was no plan. But I find it

calms pitchers down when you tell them you have one.

"What are you going to do," Eddie asked, "bend the guy's bat so he can't hit the ball?"

I looked at Eddie for a moment. Then I smiled mischievously.

Suddenly, I *did* have a plan.

"That's not a bad idea!" I said.

"No, Rod! Don't! We'll get in trouble!"

"Leave it to me."

I pulled my mask back over my face and sauntered to the plate. Bending the bat would be too obvious, I thought. Maybe if I just *moved* it slightly up or down as the caveman was swinging, it would make him foul the ball or miss it entirely. I got into my crouch.

"Nice weather we're having today," I said to the caveman as I flashed the sign for a curveball outside.

"Shut up," he replied.

Eddie put the ball right where I'd asked for it, and the caveman cocked his bat back to swing. As he brought his arms around, I focused my mind on his bat and *pulled* the bat down about a quarter of an inch. The kid fouled the ball over the bleachers in right field.

"Strike one!" boomed Winchell.

I signaled for a fastball on the inside corner of the plate. This time I used my PK to push the caveman's bat *up* a quarter of an inch as he swung. He topped the ball into the dirt.

"Strike two!" bellowed Winchell.

My PK seemed to be working. I signaled for Eddie to throw a slow ball right over the plate. He shook off the sign and looked at me like I was out of my mind. Everybody knows when you have a two-strike count on the batter you should "waste" a pitch out of the strike zone. You want him to go fishing for a bad ball.

Again, I flashed the sign for Eddie to throw it right down the pipe. If I could use my PK to mess with their bats, it wouldn't matter *where* the pitch was.

Eddie shrugged his shoulders and did as I instructed. When the caveman saw that slow ball coming right over the plate, it was like somebody had tossed a piece of raw meat at him. He pounced all over it.

But as he was bringing his bat around, I

concentrated on it and gave it a hard downward *yank*. The bat dipped just under the ball and the caveman hit nothing but air.

"Strike three!" boomed Winchell. "Yer out!"

I went out to the mound to share a laugh with Eddie.

"It worked!" he whispered, trying hard to conceal his delight. "It actually worked!"

"I *told* you I had a plan," I said with a smirk. "Okay, that's one out. We still have the runner on first to worry about. If we can get a ground ball now, we might be able to turn a double play and end the game. Just throw it right down the middle and leave the rest to me."

"Whatever you say," said Eddie.

A bat is round, of course, and so is a baseball. So if the bat hits the ball right in the center, the result is a line drive. If the bat hits the ball slightly *below* the center, the ball will go up — a fly ball. If the bat hits the ball slightly *above* the center, the ball will go down — a grounder.

That's what I wanted, a nice, easy grounder. I would push the bat up to make sure I got one.

"Hey Winch," I said to the ump as we waited for the next hitter to come from the Bomber bench. "How'd you like to see us wrap this game up right now with a double play?"

"I wish you could do it," he replied. "I gotta get home early tonight."

The next hitter approached the plate and took a few practice swings.

"Nice weather we've been having," I said to her.

"Shut up," she said.

Eddie looked in for a sign even though we both knew he was going to put the ball right over the plate. He threw it in there and the girl took a rip at it. I pushed her bat up just enough for her to hit the top of the ball.

The ball one-hopped right back to Eddie. He grabbed it, whirled around, and threw to second. Our second baseman, Toni Cippriate, caught it, tapped the base with her foot, and whipped it over to Dom Struthern at first.

Double play! Three outs. Game over. Tornadoes win!

"Your wish is my command," I called to Winchell as we walked off the field. He stared at me like I was a magician who had just made an elephant disappear before his eyes.

Chapter 9

Worst to First

The more I practiced my PK, the better I got at it. When I monkeyed with our opponents' bats, Eddie looked like Sandy Koufax, Tom Seaver, and Cy Young all rolled into one. Hitters couldn't figure out why pitches that looked so slow were so difficult to hit.

After a few games, I realized that I could not only mess up our opponents' hitting, I could also improve my *teammates'* hitting. By carefully adjusting our bats up, down, faster, or slower, I could turn our swinging strikes into singles and doubles. I could turn our foul pops into screaming line drives. We began to hit like Hall of Famers.

I had that weird vibrating feeling in the back of my head all the time, but I figured it was worth it if it gave me PK. The Tornadoes climbed out of last place and started tearing up the league. Soon we were nipping at the heels of the first place Hurricanes.

We had just won our fourth game in a row. I was collecting my gear when Sonny Day came up from behind and threw an arm around my shoulder.

"Have you been avoiding me, Rod?" he asked pleasantly.

"No," I lied, pulling his arm off me.

"Your Tornadoes are certainly doing quite well recently."

"Yes, we are."

"It's strange how your team used to be the worst in the league," he said. "Then you got hit by lightning and the Tornadoes are challenging my son Claude's Hurricanes for the pennant."

"Yeah," I said, putting my mitt in my bag. "I guess it's one of those strange coincidences."

"Your pitcher Eddie Fegson has great stuff all of a sudden. Nobody seems to be able to hit him."

"Yup," I replied. I knew what Sonny was driving at.

"It wouldn't have anything to do with your PK, would it?" he asked.

49

"Eddie's developed a secret pitch," I lied.

"Rod," Sonny said, with a harder edge to his voice, "you and I both know Eddie Fegson can't pitch his way out of a paper bag. I'm onto your tricks. You're using PK to move the bats so your team can win!"

"That's ridiculous!" I protested, without looking Sonny in the eye.

"I saw how you bent the key to my office door, Rod. You've got power in your brain. You may have more PK than anyone *ever* had."

"I don't know what you're talking about."

"Rod, I can't blame you for using your PK to help your team. But don't waste your power on a silly baseball game. You have a rare gift. It's your duty as a citizen to share it with the world. Work with *me*, and together we can harness the powers of lightning. We can solve the earth's energy problems. We can end wars. We can —"

"Rule the world?" I interrupted. "Look, Mr. Powers, I don't want to play God. I just want to play ball."

"But you and I —"

"If you want to rule the world, go ahead," I told him. "Go find a thunderstorm and let a hundred

50

and twenty-five million volts shoot through *your* body. See what it feels like."

Sonny looked at me for a moment or two, as if he was thinking about what I'd just said.

"If you won't share your PK with me," he warned, "I'm going to have to *take* it from you."

"And how are you going to do that?"

"Oh, I'll figure out a way," he said darkly. "I have a plan."

Then he stormed away.

Sticks and Stones

The Tornadoes kept winning, thanks to me and my PK. When the season ended, we surprised everybody by finishing with the same exact record as the Hurricanes.

In the history of St. Cloud Little League baseball, there had never been a tie for the pennant. The coaches weren't sure how to handle it.

They sent a flyer around asking the kids on both teams which we would prefer: Either the Tornadoes and the Hurricanes could share the championship of St. Cloud, or we could play one more game to determine the one, true champion.

The vote was unanimous. Everybody wanted to play one last game for the pennant. The game was scheduled for the Saturday after school let out for the summer.

The school year couldn't be finished quick enough, as far as I was concerned. Ever since the lightning incident, I was having a hard time in class.

Word had gotten around about what happened to me. You know how some kids are. They make fun of you if you're really fat. Or really skinny. Or tall or short. They make fun of you because of the way you dress. They're always looking for something, *anything* they can use to make fun of you.

Nobody said anything at first. But after I appeared on Channel 6 news, I noticed some kids at school looking at me and whispering. A couple of times I sat down in the lunchroom and the kid sitting nearest to me on the bench slid over a little.

Kids didn't want to touch me. It was stupid, but I guess they were afraid they might get a shock or get electrocuted or something.

They made me feel like I had a disease, like they were afraid they could catch it from me. There are two kids in the school who have cerebral palsy, and it made me feel sorry for them knowing some jerks probably treat them the same way.

Little embarrassing things started happening. We were learning about electricity in science class and Mrs. Yankell started talking about the time Benjamin Franklin sent a kite up in a thunderstorm so it could be hit by lightning. Everybody looked at me and started snickering. I felt like hiding inside my desk.

That same day we were in the auditorium for assembly. As soon as the lights were turned off, something hit me on the back of the head. Afterward, I found a paper clip on the floor. Some jerk, I suppose, thought it would be funny to throw a paper clip at my head to see if it would stick. Like I was a human magnet or something.

I went into the boys' room one day and I saw somebody had scribbled this in a stall . . .

Q: *What is Rod's favorite kind of music?*
A: *Heavy metal!*

Actually, I thought that was pretty funny, but sad at the same time. Big guys like me are usually the ones who make fun of *other* kids. I wasn't used to being picked on, and it really hurt.

When the last day of school arrived, I was really ready for summer vacation.

On that last day, I was in science class when Claude Powers came in late lugging his latest goofy invention. It was a machine about the size and shape of a roll of paper towels. There was a grip attached to the bottom, sort of like the handle of a gun. It looked like Claude had made the thing out of parts he'd salvaged from an old computer.

"It's a radar gun," Claude told Mrs. Yankell.

If you're a baseball fan, you know what a radar gun is. If you're not, it's this handheld device they point toward the pitcher as he releases the ball. It registers how fast the pitch is thrown.

Scouts use a radar gun to see if a young prospect has a big league fastball. Managers use them to see if their pitchers are getting tired. They use them on TV because fans like to know how hard the pitcher is throwing.

"Tell us how your invention works, Claude," suggested Mrs. Yankell.

"Basically, a radar gun shoots out a microwave beam and bounces it off the moving baseball,"

Claude explained. "When the microwave returns to the gun, the gun calculates how fast the ball was moving based on the difference in frequency between the beam that went out and the beam that came back."

Man, nobody should be allowed to be that smart, I thought. I didn't exactly know what Claude was talking about, but it sounded good. The only thing *I* knew about microwaves was that they were good for making popcorn.

Mrs. Yankell suggested we get a baseball from the gym and see if the gun could register its speed. But Claude didn't seem like he wanted to put on a demonstration.

"I still have a few bugs to work out," Claude said as he packed up the gun. "But I'll have it ready in time for the game tomorrow."

I noticed he glanced at me as he said that.

Chapter 11

The Big Game

The day after school ends is the best day of the year, I say. You wake up in your bed and realize you have the whole summer ahead of you.

The sky was clear when I woke up that Saturday morning. I flipped on the radio to check the weather report — hot, humid, and hazy with the chance of a late-afternoon thunderstorm.

We will have won the pennant by then, I thought.

By the time I put on my uniform, ate breakfast, and biked over to the Little League field, the bleachers were almost filled up with people. There was an atmosphere of excitement on the field that I had never seen at our games.

"Twisters! Twisters! We're gonna give you

blisters!" chanted some of the Tornado fans along the left field line.

"Hurricanes! Hurricanes! You're gonna need some Novacain!" responded the Hurricane fans along the right field line.

"Nice turnout," umpire Winchell said to me as I went out to toss grounders to our infielders.

About five feet behind home plate and a few feet off to the side, Sonny Day Powers and Claude were busily setting up Claude's radar gun. They mounted it on a homemade wooden tripod and pointed it toward home plate. I didn't say anything to Sonny, and he didn't say anything to me.

"What's that contraption, Sonny?" asked Winchell. "Whaddaya gonna do, broadcast the weather right from the field?"

"It's a radar gun, Winch," Sonny informed him. "It will tell us how fast the pitches are moving."

"Gee, I don't know, Sonny," Winch said, shaking his head. "I gotta check the league rule book to see what it says about unnecessary equipment on the field."

"Oh, come on, Winch! My son Claude made it as a science project. Give the kid a break."

"Can't you set it up behind the backstop?"

"It's not powerful enough," Sonny explained. "It's got to be right behind the plate or it won't work."

"Well, okay," said Winchell. "Just don't let it interfere with the game."

"We won't," Claude said, shooting a look at his dad.

The Hurricanes lined up along the first baseline, and the Tornadoes lined up along the third baseline. Some kids in our school band played the national anthem. When everybody reached the point where you sing, "*the la-hand of the freeeeee, and the home . . . of the . . . braaaave,*" Winch turned around to face the crowd.

"All right, let's play ball!"

The Tornadoes took the field with a big whoop. Having gone from last place to a tie for first, we were psyched. I went out to check Steady Eddie's confidence level.

"How do you feel, Ed-man?" I asked him.

"Like a million bucks," he said. "Let's blow these Hurricanes out to sea."

Eddie sure had changed since we started winning. He used to go out to the mound expecting to get hammered. Now he was sounding like he couldn't lose.

I crouched behind the plate and the first Hurricane hitter dug his spikes into the batter's box. Eddie whipped strike one over and the game was underway.

"Hey, Sonny," Winch asked, "how fast did you clock that pitch?"

"I don't know," Sonny replied, fiddling with the machine. "I'm having some trouble adjusting the gun."

Eddie struck out the side in the first inning, with a lot of help from me moving the Hurricane bats up or down to make them miss the ball. We picked up a run in our half of the inning on a couple of hits and a Hurricane error.

So it was 1–0, Tornadoes.

Eddie cruised along, mowing down the Hurricanes like they were playing baseball for the first time. I jiggled their bats so much, they couldn't hit a loud foul.

That is, unless I *let* them. Every inning or so, I would let a Hurricane get a cheap single so it wouldn't be too obvious that I was controlling their bats. One of the Hurricanes who singled

61

managed to steal second base, but I bore down and didn't let them score a run.

Meanwhile, the Tornadoes built up a lead. We scored a run in the second inning, two in the third, and another run in the fourth. That made the score 5–0. I drove in a couple of those runs myself, with a double off the left field wall.

Things were looking very good for the Tornadoes.

Every so often Winch would turn his head around and ask Sonny how fast the last pitch was. Sonny was still fussing with Claude's machine, clearly becoming more frustrated as the game went on. He kept muttering about how hard it was to adjust the microwave beam.

It got to be a bit of a joke, and soon Winch was making fun of Sonny and his machine.

"Hey, Sonny," he cracked in the fifth inning, "if that thing can't clock a pitch, maybe you can use it to bake us some potatoes!"

Sonny wasn't laughing. He just kept working on the machine, poking a screwdriver into it as the game went on. Finally, at the end of the fifth inning, Sonny exclaimed gleefully, "Eureka! I fixed it!"

Chapter 12

When It Rains, It Pours

Around that time I noticed some clouds gathering in the distance.

Storm clouds.

Maybe getting hit by lightning made me more sensitive to the weather than other people. I'm not sure. But suddenly I had a sense that something was happening. The air was changing. Nobody else seemed to notice.

A squirrel scampered around behind the backstop. It seemed more jittery than you would expect.

Way off in the distance, I thought I spotted a flash of lightning. I started counting to myself. *1 . . . 2 . . . 3 . . . 4 . . . 5 . . . 6 . . . 7 . . . 8 . . .*

9 . . . 10 . . . 11 . . . 12 . . . 13 . . . 14 . . . Then there was a low rumble of thunder.

I did a quick calculation. If it takes five seconds for the sound of thunder to travel a mile — five into fifteen is three — then the storm was three miles away.

If rain was heading in our direction, Winch might have to call the game. We had a comfortable 5–0 lead. But if the Hurricanes somehow managed to score a few runs, a good downpour would be just what we'd need to stop their rally and hold our lead.

Claude Day led off the sixth, and last, inning for the Hurricanes.

"Slam it, Claude!" said Sonny from behind the plate where he was manning his gun.

Eddie and I both knew Claude couldn't hit a pitched baseball if he were swinging a paddle. But we weren't taking any chances. On the first pitch, I was ready to jiggle his bat anyway.

Claude looked the pitch over and decided not to swing at it.

"Strike one!" announced Winch.

As I threw the ball back to Eddie, I noticed something disturbing. For the first time since I was struck by lightning, the vibrating sensation in the back of my head was gone.

It felt good to be back to normal again, but I was worried. If I didn't have that funny feeling in the back of my head, chances were I didn't have the power of PK anymore either. I went out to the mound to talk it over with Eddie.

"I don't feel anything," I said, almost in a panic. "I think my PK may be gone."

"Don't worry!" Eddie said reassuringly. "You're imagining things. Get back behind the plate and let's finish these creeps off."

That's a switch, I thought. *Eddie giving me a pep talk.*

I went back to my position and flashed the sign for a fastball on the outside part of the plate. I decided to slow down Claude's bat. That should make him swing late and miss the pitch.

Eddie put the ball right where I asked for it and Claude took a rip at it. I concentrated on his bat, but the usual pull wasn't there.

Craaaackkk!

Claude connected, and the ball soared off on a high arc toward right field. We all watched it as it disappeared over the wall.

Home run. Tornadoes 5. Hurricanes 1.

"Man!" marveled Winch, as Claude began his home run trot. "You really *smoked* that one, Claude!"

As Claude danced around the bases like a little kid on Christmas morning, the wheels in my head were turning. That might have been the first time Claude hit a ball out of the *infield*. It didn't make sense that he would suddenly be able to park one over the wall.

Was it just luck? Or something else?

One thing was for sure. I didn't have my PK anymore. Now I would *really* have to use my head.

After Claude circled the bases, he and Sonny hugged each other. Then, before going to the bench to slap hands with his teammates, Claude leaned over and planted a kiss on the radar gun.

Aha!

Suddenly I got the picture. That was no radar gun that Claude invented. I didn't know how the machine worked, but Sonny and Claude must have discovered a way — using microwaves, a magnetic field, or *something* — to suck the power of PK away from me and give it to Claude.

Sonny *told* me he would figure out a way to take my PK away, and he *did*.

What a dirty trick!

Of course, it was pretty slimy of *me* to be using PK to win baseball games in the first place. But I wasn't thinking about that at the moment. I was thinking about how the Tornadoes could possibly win the game if the Hurricanes had PK and we didn't.

I watched Claude as he told his teammates how he hit the home run. Sonny caught my eye and grinned at me.

"We're still gonna win," I muttered to him as I put my mask on.

"I don't think so," Sonny chuckled. "Without PK, the Tornadoes are a last-place team, and you know it, Rod."

He was right, of course. Eddie was furiously waving for me to come out to the mound.

"You lost it, didn't you?" he asked frantically. "You lost the power!"

"It's gone," I admitted. "I can't feel a thing."

"What are we gonna do *now?*" Eddie moaned. "You know I can't get these guys out on my own."

"I've got a plan," I said.

"What's the plan?"

"I need you to stall for time."

"What will that do?" Eddie asked.

"A storm is coming our way," I explained. "If you stall long enough, maybe the game will get rained out before they tie the score."

"*That's* your plan?" Eddie asked, disbelieving. "To hope for a *rainout*?"

"Have you got a better plan?" I said curtly.

"No."

"Then hurry up and start stalling."

"What should I do?" Eddie asked.

"Anything!" I replied. "Rub up the ball. Pick lint off your uniform. Scratch yourself. Spit. You know, like the big leaguers do."

The next Hurricane hitter took his place in the batter's box. Eddie rubbed up the ball. He picked lint off his uniform. He scratched himself. He spat. He smoothed the dirt on the mound. He dug mud out of his spikes. He took off his shoes one at a time and retied them.

It didn't look like the storm was getting any closer. And the longer Eddie stalled, the more antsy Winch became.

"That's enough, Eddie!" Winch finally shouted.

"Throw a pitch right now or forfeit the game to the Hurricanes!"

I set my mitt up over the outside corner, but Eddie's pitch was so far off the plate, even Winch couldn't call it a strike. Eddie threw the next pitch way outside too. He ended up walking the batter on four pitches.

From the corner of my eye, in the distance, I saw another flash of lightning.

I counted, *1 . . . 2 . . . 3 . . . 4 . . . 5 . . . 6 . . . 7 . . . 8 . . . 9 . . .* Then there was a crack of thunder. Five into ten is two. The storm was two miles away.

Good, I thought silently. *It's moving toward us. If it gets here fast enough, Winch will call the game before the Hurricanes can score five runs. Hurry up, storm. Get over here.*

When Eddie walked the next Hurricane hitter on four straight pitches, there were a few boos from the bleachers.

"Get it over the plate!" somebody shouted.

But Eddie walked the next guy on four pitches, too. That loaded the bases. I went out to the mound for a chitchat.

"What's the matter?" I asked Eddie. "What happened to your world-famous pinpoint control?"

"I still have it," Eddie said. "I'm just afraid that if I throw a pitch over the plate, they're going to kill it!"

"Well, you've *got* to throw strikes now," I explained, gesturing to the runners on first, second, and third. "We have no place to put this guy."

I went back to my position. Eddie fidgeted on the mound as the next Hurricane stepped up to the plate. I flashed Eddie the sign for a fastball and put my glove right over the heart of the plate. He shrugged, and then went into his windup.

It was Eddie's usual wimpy fastball. Without my PK, I couldn't do anything to help it. The Hurricane hitter smashed the ball right back at Eddie. It almost took his head off, but he dove out of the way. The runners took off from first, second, and third as soon as the ball shot past the infield.

Our center fielder, Ted Litua, was in position to field the ball and hold the hitter to a single. But the ball was hit so hard Ted didn't get his glove down fast enough. The ball skipped between his legs and rolled all the way to the fence.

71

The Hurricanes were dashing around the base paths like it was a relay race. Ted recovered quickly and retrieved the ball, but not until three Hurricanes had scored. The guy who hit the ball slid safely into third base in a cloud of dust.

That made the score 5–4. The tying run was at third, the winning run at the plate. Nobody out. Things were getting desperate for the Tornadoes.

I looked up in the sky. The storm cloud was still in the distance.

"Nice weather we're having, isn't it, Rod?" Sonny said sarcastically from behind me where he was working Claude's machine. "Still think the Tornadoes can win?"

"Shut up!" I barked.

Eddie brushed the dirt off his uniform. After that last hit, he was truly terrified of putting the ball over the plate. He walked the next two Hurricane batters to load the bases again. The Hurricanes had batted around the order, and Claude was putting on his batting helmet and gloves.

"What's the matter, Rod?" Sonny taunted me. "Is Eddie having control problems?"

Sonny was really getting on my nerves. But he also gave me an idea.

Strike Two

"We're dead," Eddie complained as I approached the mound.

"No we're not," I said. "I've got a plan."

"I hope it's better than your last plan," Eddie said, depressed.

"It is," I replied. "See that stupid machine Sonny's standing behind?"

"Yeah."

"Do you think you can hit it with a pitch?"

Eddie looked toward the machine, where Sonny was talking with Claude.

"I think so," Eddie said.

"Well, *know* so. On the first pitch, I want you to ignore Claude and knock that stupid machine over."

"Hit the gun?" Eddie put his glove over his mouth to conceal his grin.

"Yeah. Waste it. Really take it out."

"I don't throw very hard," Eddie said.

"That's okay," I assured him. "Sonny's got the whole thing on a homemade stand. One good hit and it'll collapse."

"What if I miss it?"

"If you miss it, it's a wild pitch and the runner on third will score the tying run. If you hit it, I'll be able to pick up the ball before the runners can advance. So *hit* it."

I trotted back to the plate and got into my crouch. I flashed some bogus signals to keep the Hurricanes guessing. Eddie wound up and let fly.

The ball sailed past me and I didn't try to catch it. Sonny ducked out of the way when he saw the ball coming right at him and the machine. It hit the machine with a loud *thunk*.

"Oops!" shouted Eddie, "that pitch got away from me."

Quickly, I rushed over to pick up the ball before the runners could advance.

"Ball one!" called Winchell.

Claude dropped his bat and dashed over to his machine in a panic. "My gun!" wailed Claude. "It's ruined!"

"Tough break," I said to Sonny and Claude as they picked some busted computer chips off the ground. "And just when you got the thing working."

"He did that on purpose!" Sonny complained to Winchell. "We're playing this game under protest!"

"Put a sock in it, Sonny," Winch said. "Accidents happen. The pitcher's having trouble finding the plate. He had no reason to hit your kid's radar gun. It shouldn't have been on the field to begin with."

Sonny sulked back to the Hurricane bench with what was left of his machine. I trotted out to the mound.

"That was beautiful!" I said, patting Eddie on the back. "You totally trashed it. Now let's strike Claude out. He can't hit to save his life."

"He hit a homer last time up," Eddie pointed out.

"Yeah, but that was thanks to his stupid machine. Without it, he's just a nerd with a bat."

So now everything was fair and square. Claude couldn't hit. Eddie couldn't pitch. They say good pitching will always beat good hitting. If *bad* pitching will beat bad hitting, we should be able to get Claude out.

This was baseball the way it was *supposed* to be played, I thought. Nobody had weird powers working for them. Nobody had an unfair advantage. Even though we were in deep trouble with the bases loaded and nobody out, something felt undeniably *good* about the situation.

Claude wrapped his hands around the bat, dug in at the plate, and spat on the ground. Eddie turned the ball in his hand until he found the right seam to put his fingertips on. He looked to me for the sign. I flashed fastball, low.

The pitch was in the dirt. Ball one. The next one was a little high. Ball two.

"Hey, Claude!" I said as I returned the ball to Eddie. "What are you doing after the game?"

"Goin' out for pizza with my dad."

"No you're not," I stated flatly as I signaled for a curve.

Claude looked at me as Eddie whipped the next pitch over.

"Strike one!" yelled Winch. The count was 2–1.

"See those storm clouds?" I said to Claude as I flashed the next sign. "After the game, your dad's going to take you out and play Benjamin Franklin with you. He's going to try to get you both hit by lightning."

"You're nuts!" Claude hissed. He took a big cut at the next pitch and missed it. The count was 2–2.

I didn't really think Sonny Day Powers was crazy enough to actually try and get hit by lightning, of course. But I figured if I could rattle Claude enough, he might lose his concentration. With a little luck, Eddie would strike him out.

Baseball is a tough game. You've got to use any edge you can get.

"I should punch you out," Claude muttered as he dug in for the next pitch.

"But you won't," I told Claude. "Because you know I'm right. Your dad is a nutcase. He should be locked up where he can't hurt himself or anybody else."

"Stop gabbing, you two!" Winch shouted. "Let's finish this thing!"

Clouds were starting to billow overhead. There was another lightning flash. I counted, *1* . . . *2* . . . *3* . . . I didn't even get to five before the thunder cracked. The storm was less than a mile away.

Eddie's curveball bounced in the dirt and I blocked it. The count was full, three balls and two strikes.

"Aren't you afraid of getting hit by lightning again?" Winch asked me, looking nervously at the dark cloud overhead.

"Nah," I said. "Everybody knows lightning never strikes the same place twice."

"That's only 'cause after it strikes a place," Winch said, "that place ain't *there* no more."

A True Weatherman
to the Very End

This was the moment of truth. We had a 5–4 lead in the last inning. The bases were loaded. Eddie had a full count on Claude.

As Eddie was about to start his windup, the sky over the field turned dark. It looked like it was nighttime. The air was suddenly cold, and the wind picked up. I smelled sulfur. The hair on my arms was standing up. Rain started coming down in sheets.

"That's it!" shouted Winch, holding up his hands before Eddie could deliver the pitch. "That's the ballgame! Tornadoes 5, Hurricanes 4. Let's get off the field, everybody!"

"What?" complained Claude. "This is our

chance to win the pennant! You can't call the game now! I've still got one strike!"

"It'll be a lightning strike if you don't get off the field this instant," said Winch.

"We win!" shouted Eddie. All the Tornadoes ran out to the pitcher's mound and piled on top of him.

"Get off the mound!" I yelled to my team-mates. "Lightning always strikes the highest point in a field!"

I expected Sonny Day Powers to put up an argument with Winch over calling the game, but he didn't. He was just standing near home plate staring intently at the bottom of the thundercloud.

"Dad," Claude said, tugging at Sonny's sleeve, "we better get the machine out of the rain or we'll never be able to repair it."

"Forget about the machine, Claude! Grab a bat! Come with me!"

Sonny picked up a bat and started climbing the backstop — the same backstop I climbed when I was hit by lightning. He got to the top and started waving the bat in the air as high as he could stretch his arm.

He is truly insane, I thought. *He really did want to get hit by lightning!*

81

"Sonny!" Winch shouted over the howling wind. "Come down from there! You'll get yourself killed!"

"Killed?" Sonny shouted back. "It will make me more *alive*! Claude, join me! We'll rule the world together!"

Claude took a step toward his dad, but I wrapped my arms around him and tackled him.

"Claude, don't!" I said.

Sonny was up on the top of the backstop, a human lightning rod, waving the bat back and forth.

"Find me, oh, bolt of psychokinetic power!" he hollered over the howling wind. "I am waiting for you!"

"Sonny! Don't be crazy!" Winch screamed.

"Crazy?" cackled Sonny. "Was Thomas Edison crazy when he turned electricity into incandescent light? Was Alexander Graham Bell crazy when he turned electricity into a human voice on a wire?"

"They didn't try to get hit by lightning!" Winch replied.

"They *would* have if they'd known how to harness its power!" Sonny yelled. "In the words of

83

the great philosopher Friedrich Wilhelm Nietzsche, 'I want to teach men the sense of their existence, which is the Superman, the lightning out of the dark cloud man'!"

That's when the bolt of lightning leaped out of the sky and hit Sonny Day Powers.

It's very painful to describe what happened to Sonny Day Powers when the lightning hit him. It was a pretty awesome sight, that's for sure. If I hadn't seen it with my own eyes, I don't think I would have believed it.

I don't think I should go into too much detail. Your younger brother or sister might pick up this book, and I don't want to frighten them.

Let me see. How can I put this in a way that lets you know what happened to Sonny without getting too graphic?

Okay, I think I've got it.

After the lightning bolt leaped out of the cloud at the Little League field that day, we didn't call Sonny Day Powers "Sonny" anymore.

From that moment on, he had a new name.

Partly Sonny.

He was a true weatherman to the very end.

Note to the reader

In the time it takes you to read this sentence, more than five hundred bolts of lightning will strike the earth. So if you finished the whole sentence, none of them hit you.

The ancient Greeks thought lightning was hurled down at them by angry gods. Other early civilizations believed lightning was burning wind. It wasn't until Benjamin Franklin's famous kite experiment in 1752 that lightning was shown to be a form of electricity.

In the United States, lightning is most common in the Southeastern Gulf states such as Florida and least common in the Northwest. This is because heat and humidity are the best breeding grounds for lightning.

About one hundred people are killed by lightning every year in the United States. But many people do survive lightning blasts and suffer only minor injuries.

The world record for getting struck by lightning belongs to Roy C. "Dooms" Sullivan, a rancher at Shenandoah National Park. He was hit by lightning seven times between 1942 and 1969! It is said that people were so afraid of being around Sullivan that a local restaurant owner wouldn't allow him inside his restaurant during thunderstorms.

Psychokinesis, or "PK," is one of those issues that believers and scientists will probably be arguing about forever. Mentalist Uri Geller achieved worldwide fame in the 1970s by bending keys, nails, spoons, and other metal objects without physically touching them. Most scientists said Geller was just a clever magician, but many people believed he actually had the power to influence objects using only the power of his mind.

Answers

The St. Cloud Tornadoes

Rod Caisy=icy roads
Ed Fegson=dense fog
Don L. Croft=cold front
Russ Fornweil=snow flurries
Toni Cippriate=precipitation
Dom Struthern=thunderstorm
Homer Merett=thermometer
Ted Litua=altitude
Tom E. Barre=barometer